LOOKING AT PAINTINGS

Circus

Clowness, 1899
Henri de Toulouse-Lautrec, French (1864–1901)

LOOKING AT PAINTINGS

Circus

Peggy Roalf

Series Editor
Jacques Lowe

Designer
Joseph Guglietti

Hyperion Books for Children
New York

A
JACQUES LOWE
VISUAL ARTS PROJECTS
BOOK

A Jacques Lowe Visual Arts Projects Book

 For information address Hyperion Books for Children, 114 Fifth Avenue, New York, New York 10011.

Printed in Italy

FIRST EDITION

1 3 5 7 9 10 8 6 4 2

Library of Congress Catalog Number: 92-52983

ISBN: 1-56282-305-1 (trade)/1-56282-304-3 (lib. bdg.)

Original design concept by Amy Hill

Contents

To Lionel Lisbon, with love

Introduction

LOOKING AT PAINTINGS is a series of books about understanding what great artists see when they paint. Painters have found inspiration in the artistry and pageantry of the circus, with its magnificent aerialists, riotous clowns, and dancing bears. Some painters have re-created the joyous atmosphere that unfolds night after night under the big top; others have used the circus as a metaphor to express other aspects of life, even the tragedy of war.

Edgar Degas chose a dramatic point of view to re-create the experience of craning his neck to watch Miss La La perform under the gleaming gaslight of the Cirque Fernando. Henri de Toulouse-Lautrec adopted the bold graphic look of Japanese prints to depict a ringmaster urging a trick rider to speed up the action. John Steuart Curry, while traveling with America's biggest circus, captured the speed and confidence of the Flying Codonas' death-defying triple somersault. A seventeenth-century Indian artist named Bulaqi depicted two elephants displaying their battle skills in *Shah Jahan Watching an Elephant Fight*, a jewellike painting that captures the grandeur of an imperial entertainment.

Karl Hofer portrayed three solemn clowns in *Masquerade* to express his sadness during the darkest period of World War I. Max Beckmann painted bold black outlines and harsh colors in *Acrobat on Trapeze*, a self-portrait that reveals the artist's uncertainty about his fate during the Nazi takeover of Holland in the 1940s.

Great artists have transformed their vision of the circus into images of fantasy, images of delight, and sometimes, images of fear. You can look at a three-ring extravaganza or your own backyard circus and use your imagination to see like a painter.

SHAH JAHAN WATCHING AN ELEPHANT FIGHT, about 1639
Bulaqi and unknown artist, Indian (dates unknown), opaque watercolor and gold on paper, 15" x 9¼"

Elephants have inspired kings as well as painters since Hannibal attacked Rome with an army on elephants in 216 B.C. Shah Jahan, a seventeenth-century emperor of India, was thrilled by the spectacle of trumpeting pachyderms charging in battle. He often presented ceremonial elephant fights at his palace to entertain important visitors.

Shah Jahan, best known as the builder of the Taj Mahal, kept an illustrated history of his reign in an album of small paintings called a *padshah-nameh.* A team of artists, each with a special talent, created images of wars, festivals, and wildlife for the emperor's pleasure. In this picture, Bulaqi, who specialized in painting animals, immortalized two of Shah Jahan's prize elephants. He created distinctive portraits of these animals; one appears to relish the fight, whereas the other expresses the anguish of a failing defense.

Bulaqi first drew the scene with black ink and a fine brush. He covered the entire page with opaque white watercolor paint diluted enough to allow the ink drawing underneath to show through. Bulaqi then painted with rich opaque colors and real gold. The initial layer of white paint acts as a reflector, giving the colors a luminous effect. This scene has a dreamlike feeling because Bulaqi combined his memories of many different elephant fights and noble visitors into one idealized image rather than depicting a single event from observation.

The first elephant arrived in the United States in 1796 and captivated a nation that delighted in the biggest, the strongest, and the best. The favorite beast of emperors for more than two thousand years soon became the star attraction of American circuses.

PIERROT, CALLED GILLES, 1718/19

Antoine Watteau, French (1684–1721), oil on canvas, 72 ⅝" x 58 ⅞"

In 1702, Antoine Watteau left Flanders for Paris, France, with bold ambitions but meager financial resources. At first he worked in an art factory, where dozens of poorly paid artists turned out cheap religious paintings on an assembly-line basis. As his skills improved, Watteau found better painting jobs, including scenic design for the theater. By 1715 he was recognized as a master artist and applauded for his idyllic paintings that typify the art of Watteau's time: romantic scenes of courtly pleasure graced with elaborate architecture and extravagant costumes.

The monumental size and frontal pose of *Pierrot* gives this painting a modern look compared to Watteau's other work. He created a lifelike character portrait of an actor preparing to go onstage, with supporting players waiting in the background.

In *Pierrot,* Watteau created a sumptuous feast of colors and textures. He added touches of red, yellow, and umber to every hue on his palette to create a warm tone throughout this painting. With fine brushes, he created shadows tinted with yellow and mauve to depict the folds and buttons of Pierrot's doeskin jacket, which looks softer than velvet. Watteau captured light shimmering on the satin trousers with pearly highlights that emerge from pale copper shadows. He accented the warm tones in the white costume with rose ribbons on the shoes, a scarlet jacket on a background actor, and a reddish brown tone in the landscape.

Today most experts believe that Watteau painted this portrait as a theatrical poster for a friend who was a famous actor. In 1805 the rediscovery of this painting—which had disappeared from public view for nearly a hundred years after Watteau died—gave new life to Watteau's reputation as an artist.

Giovanni Domenico Tiepolo created a series of 104 ink drawings depicting a traveling company of clowns and aerialists led by a character named Pulcinella.

THE STROLLING PLAYERS, about 1793

Francisco de Goya y Lucientes, Spanish (1746–1828), oil on tin plate, 10⅞" x 12⅝"

Francisco de Goya y Lucientes struggled to achieve his artistic ambition: to become the official painter to King Charles III of Spain. At first he worked as an assistant to prominent Spanish artists; later he taught at the Royal Academy in Madrid. After twenty years his talent finally gained him acceptance in the Spanish court. In 1793, Goya took time off from painting for the king to create a series of small pictures about Spain's best-loved entertainments for his personal enjoyment.

In *The Strolling Players,* Goya transformed a romantic natural setting into a fairyland theater for a troupe of clowns and actors of the commedia dell'arte, the classical Italian theater that had become popular in Spain. He suggests a stage by painting a steep cliff for the backdrop and a block of stone for the prompter's box. The round shape of the sundial painted on the ground is echoed by a halo of pearly light in the sky that illuminates the comic skit in progress. A backlighted shrub on the rock wall focuses attention on the players below.

On the deep tones of the dwarf's costume, Goya created brilliant highlights that heighten the twilight mood of the painting.

Goya created the background in thinly painted tones of gray-green that, by contrast, emphasize the rich colors and thick textures of the costumes worn by these characters. With delicate brushstrokes, Goya gave Harlequin a clown suit of bright, multicolored patches. The dwarf is garbed in a swirl of satin stripes fit for a king. Columbine's lovely face is framed by a lace collar embellished with gleaming highlights so thickly painted that they stand up from the canvas.

Goya called this painting a caprice, a whimsical invention designed to entertain the viewer—and to please himself.

ALEG. MEN

MISS LA LA AT THE CIRQUE FERNANDO, 1879
Edgar Degas, French (1834–1917), oil on canvas, 46" x 30 ½"

The dazzling Cirque Fernando attracted all of Paris when it opened in 1877. For Edgar Degas, the rope dancers and trick riders offered a feast of movement and color matching the brilliance of the ballet and horse racing—favorite subjects of the artist. Degas was fascinated by the daring Miss La La, who twirled in the air suspended by her teeth from a rope thirty feet above the audience.

Craning his neck, Degas observed Miss La La's spectacular stunt from directly below. First he made a series of drawings from every angle to study the aerialist's spinning figure. Referring to his drawings, Degas then constructed the form of both the aerialist and the soaring space of the circus dome in this painting. *Form* is a word often confused with shape. It means all of the qualities that uniquely describe a person or object, including size, weight, color, shape, texture, tone, and movement.

James Tissot, a friend and contemporary of Degas, was inspired by a team of beautiful charioteers at the Cirque Fernando. Through the printmaking process of etching, he created precisely drawn figures, which he formed with velvety dark shadows.

Degas eliminated distracting details and reduced his palette to a few contrasting hues: pink and green, yellow and lavender. He fashioned Miss La La's costume with freely painted lavender shadows to suggest a satin texture. He painted the walls in patches of salmon pink and tan that echo the peach flesh tone of her tights. Degas painted the ribbing of the vaulted ceiling in a light green that complements the pink walls. The bright lighting scheme re-creates the theater's dazzling gaslight. With a white highlight on the rope, he dramatized the great distance between Miss La La and the ground.

In this painting, Degas created a tour de force that equals Miss La La's thrilling performance.

JUGGLERS AT THE CIRQUE FERNANDO, 1879

Pierre-Auguste Renoir, French (1841–1919), oil on canvas, 51 ¾" x 39 ⅛"

In 1879, Pierre-Auguste Renoir was deeply in debt; for two years he had paid rent on a second painting studio with a garden. He needed outdoor space to create scenes conveying the effects of natural light. To raise money Renoir now wished to attract rich Parisians for portrait commissions.

With fine overlapping ink lines called cross-hatching, Pablo Picasso depicted the powerful back of a strong man effortlessly lifting a tiny acrobat into the air.

In *Jugglers at the Cirque Fernando,* Renoir developed a painting style more realistic than he had previously employed, without compromising his artistic standards. Renoir captured the gaiety of the circus through the use of many different shades of yellow. The ground is mottled with contrasting hues of coral, green, and lavender to create a cool yellow that appears to recede in space. Lemon yellow—the brightest shade—makes the performers' shoes and hair ribbons stand out against the background. With small, nearly invisible brushstrokes, Renoir depicted the lovely faces of the young jugglers in luminous flesh tones tinted with touches of coral and lavender that echo the tones in the background.

Instead of using traditional methods of *perspective* to create a setting that looks realistic, Renoir flattened the space in this painting, thereby providing a large, uncluttered background for the two girls. He created an illusion of depth by placing five oranges in a diagonal path on the ground to lead the viewer's eyes toward the distance.

Renoir's promotional experiment was successful. When this painting was exhibited in 1879, it captivated a wealthy publisher who commissioned Renoir to paint *Madame Charpentier and Her Children.*

Renoir.

A CARNIVAL EVENING, 1886

Henri Rousseau, French (1844–1910), oil on canvas, 46" x 35 ⅛"

Henri Rousseau, who worked as a poorly paid customs clerk, was called *Le Douanier,* a French term that means "customhouse official," by his friends. These artists and poets honored him with this title out of respect for the polite little man who painted on his one day off after working a seventy-hour week.

In this imaginary scene a full moon casts silvery light on two clowns strolling under an immense sky. Although the figures and landscape seem almost as flat as paper cutouts, Rousseau created a feeling of depth by using light and dark colors. He painted the figures in pastel hues that stand out against the nearly black ground. Delicate tints of rose, blue, and gold in the distance draw the viewer's eyes from the figures into the trees, darkly silhouetted against the gossamer light.

Rousseau creates an air of mystery through the dramatic connection between the small figures and the vast, luminous sky. The pink tone glowing through the blue sky is repeated in highlights on the costumes. A pointed cloud that echoes the shape of the clown's hat forms a triangle connecting the clowns with the clouds and the moon. By emphasizing the great scale of the heavens, Rousseau created a scene that is as disquieting as an image that wakes us from a dream.

A Carnival Evening is the first painting that Le Douanier Rousseau publicly exhibited. His personal vision, expressed in magical paintings such as this one, won the admiration of his fellow artists Pablo Picasso and Paul Gauguin.

BAREBACK RIDERS, 1886

W. H. Brown, American (dates unknown), oil on cardboard, 18½" x 24½"

The first American circus performance took place in 1785 when a Philadelphia horseman named Thomas Pool presented a trick-riding exhibition that captivated the public's imagination. By 1880 several small circuses in New York State merged to form the traveling three-ring extravaganza called Barnum and Bailey's Greatest Show on Earth. W. H. Brown, a painter who lived at that time in Binghamton, New York, was inspired by an equestrian team that took acrobatic riding to daring new heights.

We know little about Brown—not even whether the artist was a man or a woman. Only four paintings signed by the artist have survived, two of which are circus scenes. In *Bareback Riders,* Brown captured the effects of theatrical lighting beneath the big top, from the clouds of smoky haze below the roof to colorful reflections bouncing off the gaily decorated tent. Through the contrast of scale and color, Brown focuses attention on an electrifying performance. The trick riders seem unusually large compared with the horse and the clown. Their outstanding balancing act is matched by the painter's skill in balancing colors. Striped bunting in the background cheerfully echoes the red, yellow, and blue in the performers' costumes; the black horse and the ringmaster's attire add an air of formality to the lively spectacle.

Brown styled the costumes with elaborate details, sharply defined compared to the faceless audience. With fine brushstrokes the artist depicted gold embroidery on the man's red suit; blue satin and lace on the woman's tutu; stars, stripes, and zigzag ruffles on the clown's pajamas.

Like other American folk artists of the nineteenth century, the almost anonymous W. H. Brown displays a brilliant technical mastery of painting in a style outside the mainstream of academic art.

WHBrown
86

IN THE CIRQUE FERNANDO: THE RINGMASTER, 1888

Henri de Toulouse-Lautrec, French (1864–1901), oil on canvas, 39 ½" x 63 ½"

As a teenager, Henri de Toulouse-Lautrec was told that he would be permanently handicapped as a result of a rare form of dwarfism. Unable to pursue a military career, a common occupation for young men of his class, Toulouse-Lautrec immersed himself in the study of painting. The glittering world of Parisian entertainments—so different from his aristocratic background—became the focus of his life and the subject of his work.

Toulouse-Lautrec adopted a method of depicting space found in the Japanese woodblock *prints* that he admired. He shaped a bold composition based on the concentric circles in the ring and grandstand of the Cirque Fernando. Like the Japanese printmakers, Toulouse-Lautrec created an illusion of depth by exaggerating the size of the performers in the foreground compared with the spectators in the distance. The ringmaster's commanding gesture sweeps the viewer's eye into the picture, which is cropped, or abruptly cut off at the edges, to spotlight a cantering horse and its rider.

Toulouse-Lautrec painted expressive shapes, lines, and flat areas of color rather than shading and highlights to create the appearance of solid forms. With sharply observed lines, he depicted the rider's slim but powerful arms and legs. He emphasized the graphic style of this painting with high-contrast black and white and a palette of muted green, mauve, and dark red.

In this painting, Toulouse-Lautrec captured the circus atmosphere in a pioneering style that, in the twentieth century, would make him one of the most admired and imitated poster artists.

Georges Rouault suggested the speed of an accomplished juggler's routine through the blurred arc of reddish brown color at the top of the picture.

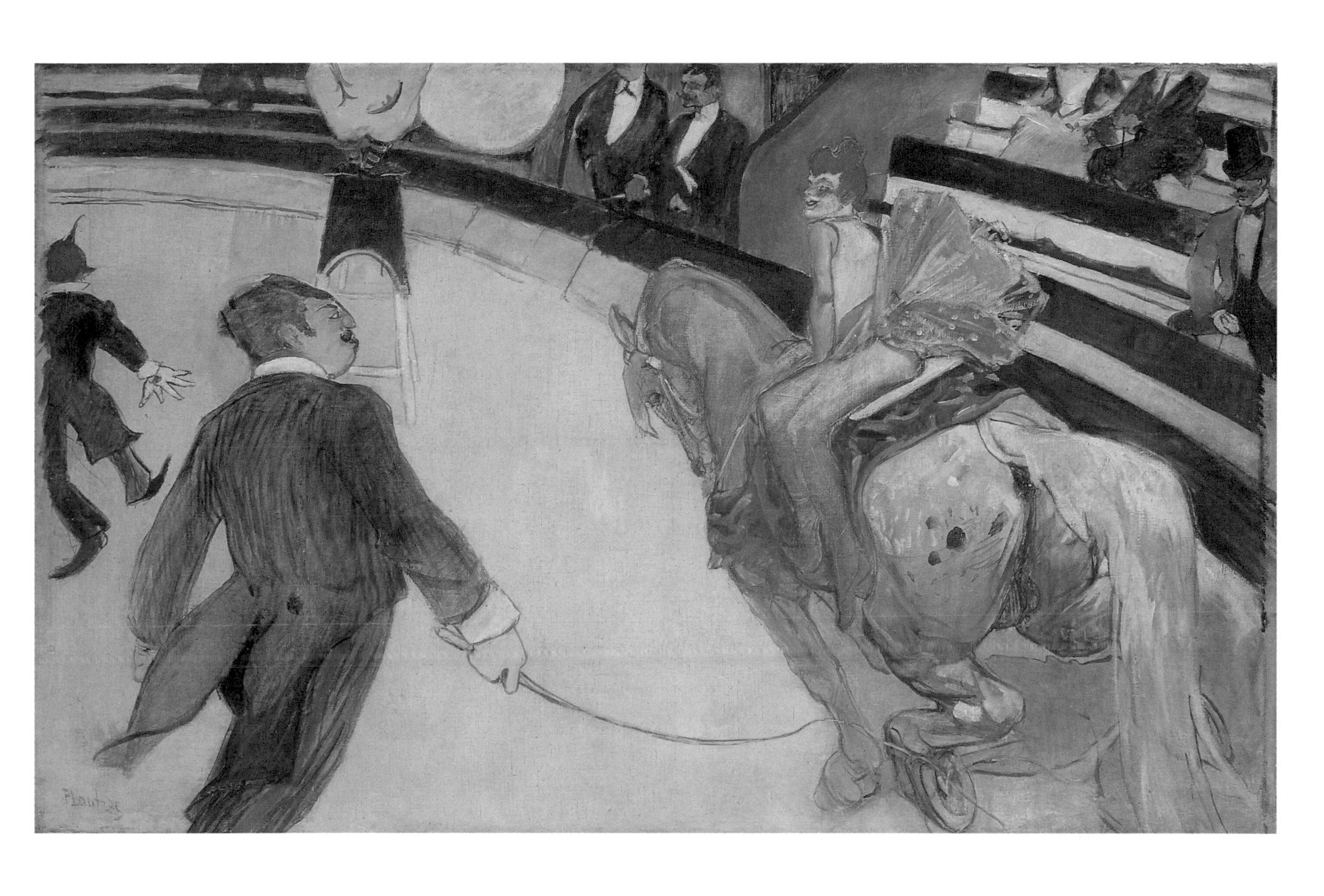

THE CIRCUS, 1891

Georges Seurat, French (1859–91), oil on canvas, 72" x 58 ¼"

Georges Seurat was fascinated by the new scientific theories of color and optics. Through his studies he developed a method of painting that was later called *pointillism*: painting with dots of color. The tiny spots of pure, unmixed color blended in the viewer's eye when seen from a few feet away. Seurat's paintings appear to be not merely pictures of light but the source of light itself. In 1886, Seurat, who had previously painted outdoor scenes, began to explore the effects of artificial light in pictures of Parisian nightlife.

Georges Seurat had a personal language of color to express different moods. To convey a happy feeling, he enlivened the spectators' dark clothes with thousands of dots of yellow.

In *The Circus*, Seurat expressed gaiety through curving, upturned forms and bright colors. All of the figures in the foreground are composed of lines sweeping upward, from the trick rider's graceful arms to the acrobat's pointed toes and crescent-shaped grin. The ringmaster's snapping whip is echoed by the clown's yellow banner that swirls out of the picture and back in again to create a feeling of movement. Seurat created many different shades of yellow by adding dots of orange, white, ocher, and blue in varying amounts. The detail (left) shows that he produced a rich golden hue by adding speckles of orange to the acrobat's costume.

Seurat contrasted the rhythmic lines and shapes of the circus performers with a background composed of horizontal bands and right angles. The motionless spectators, painted head on or from a three-quarter view, create a strong contrast with the nimble trick rider in the ring.

Seurat died two days after this painting was first exhibited in 1891. He remained unknown to the general public for many years, but, in studios around the world, other painters who admired Seurat's innovations collected reproductions of *The Circus*.

SOIR BLEU, detail, 1914
Edward Hopper, American (1882–1967), oil on canvas, 36" x 72"

Edward Hopper studied in Paris from 1909 to 1911. In his spare time he enjoyed the outdoor cafés and street life of the romantic French capital. After returning to New York, Hopper painted *Soir Bleu* from his memories of a street carnival called Mi Carême. In a scene suffused in shades of evening blue that give this painting its title, Hopper expresses the despair he felt for the French people besieged by the calamity of World War I.

In the small illustration that shows the entire painting (below), we can see a clown and an entertainer mingle with two well-dressed patrons on an outdoor terrace. Hopper created a still atmosphere drained of energy. Everyone seems absorbed in private thoughts that isolate them from one another.

Hopper gave the clown, who dominates the scene, weight and substance through broad areas of white paint marked by simple but precisely observed details. Hopper molded the clown's strong features with strokes of paint tinted with yellow and gray. A dark shadow under his nose suggests the strong light beaming down from above. Blue-gray shading separates the clown's ruffled collar and jacket into two distinct masses. In the background, empty zones of blue and gray contrast with the irregular forms on the crowded terrace. Hopper created a theatrical effect with a beam of harsh light focused on the entertainer who looms over the party.

Pretty lanterns that contrast with dark, somber colors emphasize the feeling of sadness that Edward Hopper created in Soir Bleu, *shown here in its entirety.*

As in many of his best-known paintings that depict solitary figures in shabby rooms, Hopper shows us people who seem to be waiting for something to occur. Because he shows ordinary people in everyday settings, Hopper's paintings evoke an aching feeling of strangely familiar loneliness.

MASQUERADE, 1922

Karl Hofer, German (1878–1956), oil on canvas, 50¾" x 40½"

Like other twentieth-century painters such as Max Beckmann, Karl Hofer expressed a pessimistic view of life in paintings with circus themes. During a visit to Paris at the outbreak of World War I, the German painter was confined to a detention camp and treated as an enemy of France. Hofer communicated his despair in this painting of three clowns. He identified with these jesters, whose comic skits are often tinged with sadness.

Hofer posed the three figures with the white-suited Pierrot in the middle to emphasize the contrast between dark and bright colors. He spotlighted the clowns against a blue-black background with a patch of yellow behind Harlequin, who wears a suit of multicolored diamonds. With masterful strokes of orange over wet black paint, Hofer blended the colors directly on the canvas to create the effect of velvet in Punch's costume. The artist painted broad highlights of pale blue, yellow, and mauve on Pierrot's jacket to suggest reflections on shining white satin. With the pointed end of a brush, Hofer scratched crisp outlines around the figures while the thick paint was still wet.

Although the clowns are depicted standing in place, Hofer creates a feeling of nervous energy with dynamic shapes, such as Harlequin's curved and pointed hat, that suggest motion through their directional form. The dynamic angle of Harlequin's arm leads the viewer's eye to the angular arrangement of Pierrot's hand holding a fan; the bent shape of Punch's pointed hat echoes these forms.

Hofer evokes a bittersweet mood in *Masquerade* by contrasting the clowns' woeful expressions with glorious shapes and colors in their costumes.

With pencil, George Grosz created a delicate balance between sharp geometric lines and soft shading in this drawing of a rope dancer named Lina Pantzer.

CLOWN ON A HORSE, 1927

Marc Chagall, Russian (1887–1985), gouache on paper, 26" x 20"

After the Bolshevik Revolution of 1917, Marc Chagall was appointed director of a new school of fine arts in his native city, Vitebsk, Russia. However, the new Communist government criticized Chagall's imaginative teaching methods and forced his resignation. In 1923, Chagall returned to Paris, the city where he had found success and happiness eight years earlier. Chagall thrived on his newfound artistic freedom. He created this painting as a study for a series of etchings on circus themes commissioned by Ambrose Vollard, the renowned publisher of artists' *prints*.

Like many of the figures in Chagall's paintings, this gleeful clown is immune to the laws of gravity. Chagall evokes a happy mood through the use of fanciful patterns and brilliant colors. He conveyed his love for animals through the pretty flowers that seem to grow in the horse's mane. Accents of red paint on the clown's plume, umbrella, and shoes echo the multicolor markings on the pony. Chagall creates a dream world through the surreal pink and blue cloud forms floating through the background.

Chagall used a versatile type of watercolor paint called *gouache,* which can be used in its opaque form or thinned with water to create transparent colors. The clown's yellow jacket and the deep blue background are opaque: they completely cover the paper on which the artist painted. However, Chagall diluted white paint to make transparent highlights on the ball; the blue background shows through, emphasizing its spherical form. With opaque yellow and white, and transparent green and blue, Chagall created the whimsical design on the clown's tights.

Chagall affectionately called this series of gouache paintings Vollard's Circus in honor of his friend whose continued patronage freed the artist from financial worry.

CHAGALL

PIP AND FLIP, 1932
Reginald Marsh, American (1898–1954), tempera on paper mounted on canvas, 48 ¼" x 48 ¼"

Before pursuing a career in painting, Reginald Marsh was an illustrator for magazines and newspapers. He developed great skill in drawing by observing and sketching people on the streets of New York City. Coney Island, with its circus sideshow and boardwalk, was Marsh's favorite subject. He preferred "the masses to the classes," favoring ordinary people who reveled in the cheap entertainment that could be had for a five-cent subway ride over the well-off people of his own background who enjoyed the opera.

In *Pip and Flip,* Marsh compared the earthy realism of the crowd with the lurid sideshow. The motionless, larger-than-life figures on the flat backdrop contrast strongly with the surging throng on the boardwalk. The artist anchored this dynamic composition through a triangular arrangement that comes to a point above the two dancers watching the spectators.

Through the hulking, angular pose, Walt Kuhn suggests this resting clown's weight and his fatigue.

Rather than first laying out the composition in pencil, Marsh painted directly onto the canvas, referring to drawings he had made at Coney Island. He began by modeling the forms, or making the figures appear three-dimensional, using deep gray paint to create shading. Then Marsh built up colors in thin transparent layers that allow the details of the gray underpainting to show through in the finished work. Marsh chose to work in tempera because the fast-drying paint forced him to work quickly and enabled him to maintain the lively spirit of his sketchbook drawings.

Marsh brings to life the vivid sights and sounds of Coney Island in *Pip and Flip.* The spectators become the spectacle, whereas the circus sideshow serves as a backdrop to the action.

DIAMOND
IN PERSON
PIP & FLIP
TWINS FROM PERU
MAJOR MITE
SMALLEST ENTERTAINER
ON EARTH
THE SMALLEST MAN ON EARTH
MITE The SMALLEST MAN ON EARTH

THE FLYING CODONAS, 1932

John Steuart Curry, American (1897–1946), tempera and oil on composition board, 36" x 30"

Early in his career John Steuart Curry painted scenes depicting rural American life. He was moved by the struggles of Kansas farmers against nature's fires, floods, and tornadoes. Searching for new inspiration for his work, Curry traveled with the Ringling Brothers Barnum and Bailey Circus for three months in 1932.

In this painting Curry captured the excitement of aerialist Alfredo Codona rocketing through space in a sixty-mile-per-hour triple somersault. Curry created the effect of dizzying height by selecting a view close to the ceiling of the big top. To capture the sensation of speed, he painted the Codonas in sharp detail compared to the blurred background—an effect often seen in sports photographs when the camera pans, or moves, to follow the athletes. Curry placed the two figures near the edges of the painting to emphasize the distance between aerialist and catcher as well as the danger of their death-defying feat.

Curry conveyed the dazzling theatrical lighting using bright colors accented with transparent glazes of white paint. He applied a thin layer of white over the entire ceiling and bright yellow highlights on the catcher's orange costume to suggest the heat and glare of the spotlights.

During his tour with the circus, Curry filled several sketchbooks with drawings of aerialists, clowns, and animal trainers. Later, in his studio, he used these drawings to develop a series of paintings, including this one, that depict highly trained athletes whose daredevil feats appear effortless.

John Steuart Curry encircled Clyde Beatty, the great lion tamer, with his ferocious cats to dramatize their size, power, and numbers.

JOHN STEWART CURRY

CHARIOT RACE, 1933
Milton Avery, American (1885–1965), oil on canvas, 48" x 72"

Milton Avery is known for dreamlike landscape paintings that hover between reality and abstraction. As a young man he worked at a variety of night jobs in order to paint during daylight hours. Avery's paintings glow with colors that seem to be lighted from within.

In *Chariot Race,* Avery takes the role of a fiendish impresario—an imaginary P. T. Barnum who presents a haunted circus. Two ghostly trapeze artists swing into a scene in which faceless charioteers drive their horses with invisible reins and traces. Clowns and circus animals float helter-skelter through the otherworldly spectacle.

Avery conjured up this phantom circus from his imagination and made a small watercolor to quickly put down his ideas. In this six-foot-wide oil painting, he re-created the freshness of his vision by referring to his original composition.

This detail shows a performing seal floating through the vaporous blue haze of Milton Avery's imaginary circus scene.

To achieve the luminous transparency of his watercolors Avery used oil paint diluted with turpentine. He painted the gray horse with a thin layer of purple. Over this he brushed on a slightly thicker gray, letting the purple tone show through to form shadows on the horse's legs, chest, and neck. With crisp lines he shaped its rear leg and tail. Avery used the same technique to paint the white horse and the trick rider, who is tinted with shadows created by the indigo background.

In the background, the curved horizon line defined with wispy cloudlike forms suggests that Avery's circus exists beyond the earth, beyond reality.

ACROBAT ON TRAPEZE, 1940

Max Beckmann, German (1884–1950), oil on canvas, 57 ½" x 35 ½"

After the outbreak of World War II in 1939, Max Beckmann wrote in his diary: "I begin this new notebook in a condition of complete uncertainty about my own existence and the state of our planet. Wherever one looks: chaos and disorder." Beckmann had fled to Amsterdam, Holland, to escape Nazi persecution in Germany. As Beckmann was preparing to leave for the United States, Hitler's army invaded Holland and the artist was trapped there until 1947. Beckmann created this self-portrait as a circus performer to express his nightmarish situation.

A daring acrobat perches high above the ground without a net. Painted life-size, the squatting figure nearly fills the canvas. It creates a dramatic contrast to the tiny people far below and suggests the isolation Beckmann felt while he was cut off from his own country.

Beckmann creates a mood of anxiety through a series of jagged forms and expressive brush marks. He boldly outlined the aerialist with black paint, breaking the figure into angular green, purple, and yellow shapes. Using a technique called impasto, Beckmann created rough textures in the thick surface of the paint with a palette knife and stiff brushes. He emphasized the tense atmosphere through the contrast of black shadows on the figure and a gaseous yellow background. The slanting trapeze bars suggest the swaying motion of the high-wire artist awaiting his turn to fly.

This is one of several circus paintings Beckmann created to express his belief that war is a brief, insane act in the endless drama of life.

Ben Shahn used a pen with a flexible nib to draw spirited lines that interconnect the figures of this multispecies circus.

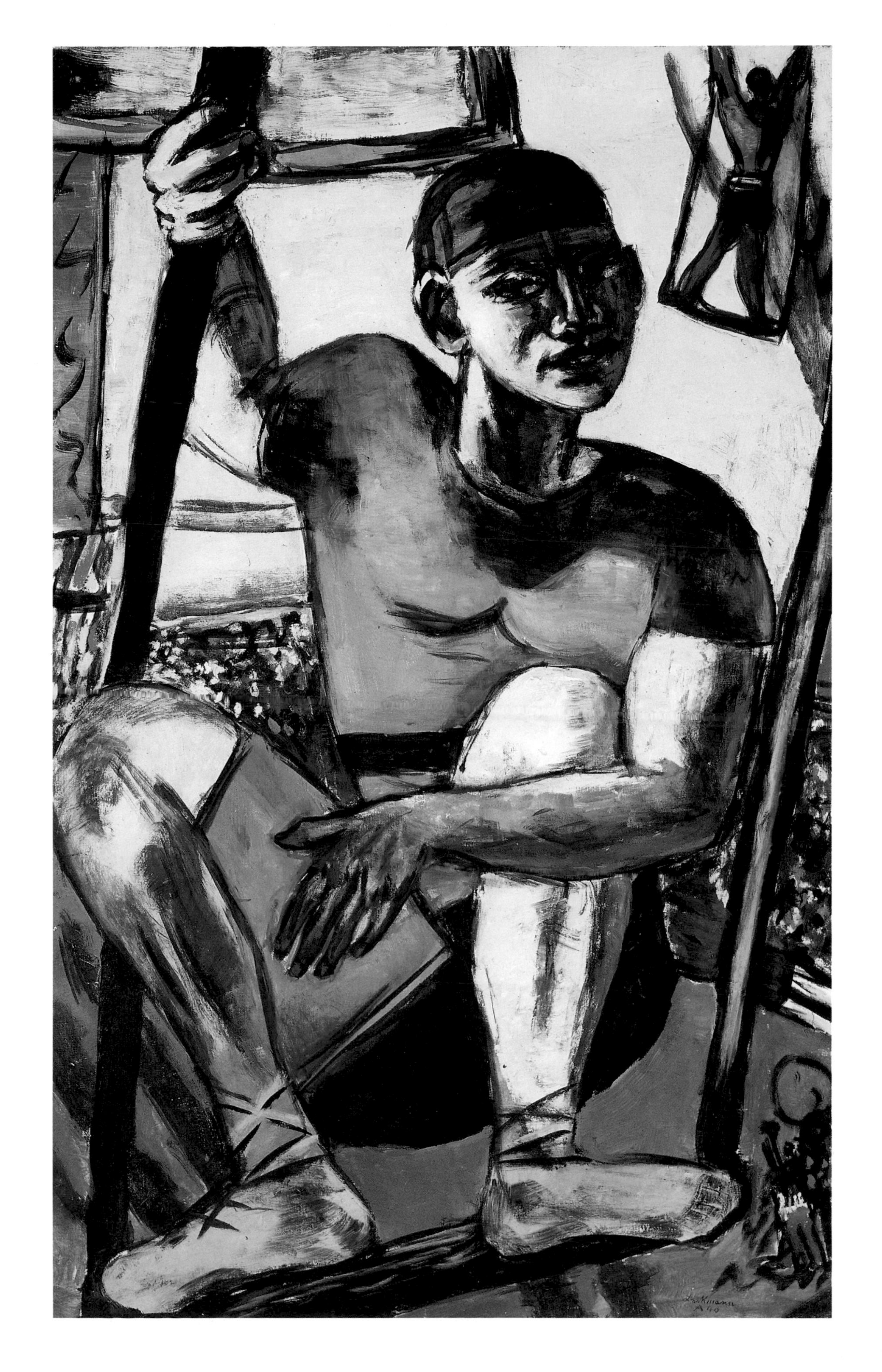

CIRCUS ELEPHANTS, 1941

John Marin, American (1870–1953), crayon and wash on paper, 18⅞" x 24⅝"

The elephant has been the mainstay of American circuses since Hackaliah Bailey brought an African elephant named Old Bet to New York in 1805. Whether leading the circus parade, lifting beautiful dancers into the air with their trunks, or raising the poles of the big top, circus elephants have inspired American painters for almost two hundred years.

John Marin, famous for seascape paintings that express the changing moods of weather through powerful abstract forms, turned to a more figurative style in 1932. He began a series of circus scenes and created this joyous celebration of the elephant.

In this painting seven pachyderms parade in the center ring. Marin focuses our attention on the animals by painting both abstract and realistic details. He suggests the human audience in the background with simple dabs of primary color, whereas the performing elephants are painted true to form. At the bottom of the picture, Marin scribbled in an audience of almost abstract elephants with dashing strokes of paint.

Robert Riggs chose a worm's-eye view to emphasize the mammoth size of this herd of dancing pachyderms.

Marin used *watercolor* in different degrees of wetness. He drew the fluid curves of the animals with brown paint and a fine wet brush. When the lines had dried, he emphasized their jumbo forms with brown and blue tones thinly diluted with water, called wash. The pale yellow ground is also painted in wash, whereas a red stroke denoting the ring and blue strokes in the foreground are formed with soft crayon. Marin suggests the excitement and constant activity of the circus through expressive curved lines and spots and spatters of color.

Marin affectionately created a playful circus of elephants performing for a front-row audience of elephants.

THREE CLOWNS IN A RING, 1944

George Schreiber, American (born 1904), watercolor on paper, 22½" x 26¾"

Madcap clowns have enchanted George Schreiber since his childhood in Belgium. After completing his training in Europe, Schreiber moved to New York City. When his daughter Joan was born in 1947, Schreiber wrote and illustrated a book for her called *Bambino the Clown*. Bambino makes a special appearance as the ringmaster in this painting, which the artist based on his memories of European clowns that romped through the audience to amuse the children.

Schreiber chose a trapeze artist's point of view for *Three Clowns in a Ring* to depict a frenzied scene: the clown on the left catapults through the air toward the ring, where eight horses race at a wild gallop. With a crack of his whip, Bambino urges the trick riders to speed up the action.

Schreiber achieved the spontaneous effect of this painting through a watercolor technique that depends upon working rapidly to keep the paper wet. He created soft shadows on Bambino's trousers by applying dark umber over wet brown paint. He left areas of paper uncovered to form the white horses and added shading and details with transparent gray. Schreiber created the effect of colorful stage lighting through a wash of brilliant red in the background. After the paper had dried, he formed the pattern on the airborne clown's shirt and the horses' feathers and bridles.

Pastel colors and musical notes skittering through the air create a feeling of fun in Jean Dufy's painting of a circus band.

In this tribute to clowns, Schreiber turns the circus over to the zany characters from his childhood who lived on in his imagination.

Schreiber '44

CLOWN WITH A PIGEON, 1989

Krishna Reddy, Indian (born 1925), color engraving on paper, 16" x 12"

Krishna Reddy sees circus clowns as artists and magicians. His love of clowns began in the small open-air theaters he enjoyed as a child in India. The performers were often friends and neighbors from his own village, taking part in the festivities and sharing the fun.

In this *print*, Reddy depicts a prankster materializing a pigeon from the air. As the members of the audience express their appreciation with a roar of applause, they become one with the world of clowns.

Yasuo Kuniyoshi created the rich black tones of this acrobat's costume by drawing with a greasy crayon onto a stone, from which he made a print called a lithograph.

Reddy conveyed his vision of clown magic by transforming a flat slab of metal into a printing plate. He carved the image with sharp tools, making expressive lines around the figures and textured patterns on the clown's jacket. Reddy also transferred photographic images onto the metal, such as the clown's hands and the bird. He then applied colored inks—red, blue, yellow, and black—to the plate. Using a printing press, Reddy created ten identical impressions onto sheets of paper.

Until Reddy developed an innovative method of printing all of his colors at once, most artists found printmaking to be a laborious process because it required a different plate for each color. Artists could not even see the results of their creativity until every color had been imposed, one plate at a time. With Reddy's technique, all of the colors are transferred from a single plate onto paper in one pass through the press. This enables him to experiment with different color effects because he can see the finished work immediately.

Reddy travels all over the world sharing his knowledge with other artists who make prints. For many painters, printmaking is a way to express their vision in multiple impressions of a single image that can be appreciated by many people.

Glossary and Index

ABSTRACT, 36, 40: Having form and color but not recognizable subject matter.
Acrobat on Trapeze, 39
ARCHITECTURE, 10: (1) A building that has been carefully designed and constructed. (2) The art of designing buildings.
Avery, Milton, 36

BACKGROUND, 10, 12, 16, 20, 24, 26, 28, 30, 34, 36, 38, 40, 42: The part of a painting behind the subject; the distant area. *See also* FOREGROUND
Bareback Riders, 21
Beckmann, Max, 38
Brown, W. H., 20
Bulaqi, 8

Carnival Evening, A, 19
Chagall, Marc, 30
Chariot Race, 37
Circus, The, 25
Circus Elephants, 41
Clown on a Horse, 31
Clown with a Pigeon, 45
COLOR, as it is used by painters, is identified by three different terms.

The actual appearance of the color (red, blue, bluish green, etc.) is its *hue*. Everyday words can be used to describe a hue that occurs in nature, such as rose, sky blue, and grass green.

A lighter or darker version of a hue, created by adding white or black, is called a *shade*.

A hue that is changed by adding a small amount of another color is a *tint*. For example, a painter might add a small amount of red to gray, to yellow, and to blue and create reddish tints of these original colors. *See also* TONE

COMMISSION, 16, 30: 1) A work of art produced at the request of a patron. 2) The appointment of an artist to create such a work of art.
COMPOSITION, 22, 32, 36. *See also* DESIGN
CONTRAST, 14, 16, 20, 22, 24, 28, 38: Big differences in light and dark, shapes, colors, and activity.
Curry, John Steuart, 34

Degas, Edgar, 14 (Pronounced Edgar Deh-gah)
DESIGN, 10, 22: (1) The arrangement of objects and figures in a painting through the combination of colors and shapes. This is also called *composition*. (2) A decorative pattern of shapes, such as leaves. *See also* COMPOSITION
DRAWING, 8, 14, 32, 34: The art of creating an image by making marks on paper. Drawings can be made using dry materials such as pencil, charcoal, and crayon or wet materials such as ink and paint. Drawings may consist of lines, tones, shading, and dots. Twentieth-century artists began to create drawings that are difficult to distinguish from paintings. An important difference is that drawings are usually on paper rather than canvas, wood, or metal. Drawings produced with more than one kind of material are known as mixed-media drawings.

Flying Codonas, The, 35
FOREGROUND, 22, 24, 40: The area in a painting closest to the viewer. *See also* BACKGROUND

Goya y Lucientes, Francisco de, 12

HIGHLIGHT, 10, 12, 14, 18, 22, 28, 30, 34: The lightest color or brightest white in a painting.
Hofer, Karl, 28
Hopper, Edward, 26

INK, 8, 44: Usually, a jet black fluid made of powdered carbon mixed with a water-soluble liquid. Ink drawings can be made with dark lines and diluted tones of gray. Inks are also made in colors.
In the Cirque Fernando: The Ringmaster, 23

Jugglers at the Cirque Fernando, 17

LINE, 22, 24, 40: A mark, such as a pencil mark, that does not include gradual shades or tones.

Marin, John, 40
Marsh, Reginald, 32
Masquerade, 29
Miss La La at the Cirque Fernando, 15

OPAQUE, 8, 30: Not letting light pass through. Opaque paints conceal what is under them. (The opposite of TRANSPARENT)

PAINT: Artists have used different kinds of paint, depending on the materials that were available to them and the effects they wished to produce in their work.

Different kinds of paint are similar in the way they are made.

1. Paint is made by combining finely powdered pigment with a vehicle. A vehicle is a fluid that evenly disperses the color. The kind of vehicle used sometimes gives the paint its name, for example: oil paint. Pigment is the raw material that gives paint its color. Pigments can be made from natural minerals and from artificial chemical compounds.
2. Paint is made thinner or thicker with a substance called a medium, which can produce a consistency like that of water or mayonnaise or peanut butter.
3. A solvent must be used by the painter to clean the paint from brushes, tools, and the hands. The solvent must be appropriate for the composition of the paint.

OIL PAINT: Pigment is combined with an oil vehicle (usually linseed or poppy oil). The medium chosen by most artists is linseed oil. The solvent is turpentine. Oil paint is never mixed with water. Oils dry slowly, enabling the artist to work on a painting for a long time. Some painters add other materials, such as pumice powder or marble dust, to produce thick layers of color. Oil paint has been used since the fifteenth century. Until the early nineteenth century, artists or their assistants ground the pigment and combined the ingredients of paint in their studios. When the flexible tin tube (like a toothpaste tube) was invented in 1840, paint made by art suppliers became available.

TEMPERA: Pigment is combined with a water-based vehicle. The paint is combined with raw egg yolk to "temper" it into a mayonnaiselike consistency usable with a brush. The solvent for tempera is water. Tempera was used by the ancient Greeks and was the favorite technique of painters during the medieval period in Europe. It is now available in tubes, ready to use. The painter supplies the egg yolk.

WATERCOLOR: Pigment is combined with gum arabic, a water-based vehicle. Water is both the medium and the solvent. Watercolor paint now comes ready to use in tubes (moist) or in cakes (dry). Watercolor paint is thinned with water, and areas of paper are often left uncovered to produce highlights.

Gouache is an opaque form of watercolor, which is also called tempera or body color.

Watercolor paint was first used 37,000 years ago by cave dwellers who created the first wall paintings.

PERSPECTIVE, 16: Perspective is a method of representing people, places, and things in a painting or drawing to make them appear solid or three-dimensional rather than flat. Six basic rules of perspective are used in Western art.

1. People in a painting appear larger when near and gradually become smaller as they get farther away.
2. People in the foreground overlap people or objects behind them.
3. People become closer together as they get farther away
4. People in the distance are closer to the top of the picture than those in the foreground.
5. Colors are brighter and shadows are stronger in the foreground. Colors and shadows are paler and softer in the background. This technique is often called *atmospheric perspective*
6. Lines that in real life are parallel (such as the line of a ceiling or the line of a floor) are drawn at an angle, and the lines meet at the *horizon line*, which represents the eye level of the artist and the viewer.

In addition, a special technique of perspective, called *foreshortening*, is used to compensate for distortion in figures and objects painted on a flat surface. For example, an artist will paint the hand of an outstretched arm larger than it is in proportion to the arm, which becomes smaller as it recedes toward the shoulder. This correction, necessary in a picture using perspective, is automatically made by the human eye observing a scene in life. *Foreshortening* refers to the representation of figures or objects, whereas perspective refers to the representation of a scene or a space.

Painters have used these methods to depict objects in space since the fifteenth century. However, many twentieth-century artists choose not to use perspective. An artist might emphasize colors, lines, or shapes to express an idea instead of showing people or objects in a realistic space.

Pierrot, Called Gilles, 11

Pip and Flip, 33

PORTRAIT, 8, 10, 16, 38: A painting, drawing, sculpture, or photograph that represents an individual's appearance and, usually, his or her personality.

PRINT, 7, 14, 22, 30, 44: One of multiple images created by mechanical means from the same original. Prints can be made from a metal plate (etching, aquatint, engraving), from a woodblock (wood engraving, wood-block print), from silk gauze (silkscreen print), or from a stone (lithograph). Etchings are traditionally made using a flat sheet of copper called a plate. The artist first covers the plate with a resinous material called *ground*. He then draws lines with a pointed metal tool to expose the metal plate under the ground. The plate is immersed in a vat of acid which bites, or etches, lines into the metal in areas not covered with ground. The artist then inks the plate with a roller and, using a printing press, imposes the same image onto many sheets of paper. In the twentieth century, artists have developed new printmaking methods, often using photographic processes and sometimes carving lines and textures directly onto the plate.

Reddy, Krishna, 44

Renoir, Pierre-Auguste, 16 (Pronounced Ruhn-wahr)

Rousseau, Henri, 18 (Pronounced Ahn-ri Roo-so)

Schreiber, George, 42

Seurat, Georges, 24 (Pronounced Zhor-zeh Suh-rah)

SHADOW, 10, 26, 36, 38, 42: An area made darker than its surroundings because direct light does not reach it.

Shah Jahan Watching an Elephant Fight, 9

Soir Bleu, 27

Strolling Players, The, 13

Three Clowns in a Ring, 43

TONE, 10, 12, 14, 18, 36, 40: The sensation of an overall coloration in a painting. For example, an artist might begin by painting the entire picture in shades of greenish gray. After more colors are applied using transparent glazes, shadows, and highlights, the mass of greenish gray color underneath will show through and create an even tone, or *tonal harmony*.

One of the ways that painters working with opaque colors can achieve the same effect is by adding one color, such as green, to every other color on their palette. This makes all of the colors seem more alike, or harmonious. The effect of tonal harmony is part of the artist's vision and begins with the first brushstrokes. It cannot be added to a finished painting. *See also* COLOR

Toulouse-Lautrec, Henri de, 22

TRANSPARENT, 30, 32, 34, 36, 42: Allowing light to pass through so colors underneath can be seen. (The opposite of OPAQUE)

Watteau, Antoine, 10 (Pronounced Ahn-twan Wat-toe)

Credits

Frontispiece

CLOWNESS, 1899
Henri de Toulouse-Lautrec, French
Colored pencil sketch, 14" x 10"

Page

9 *SHAH JAHAN WATCHING AN ELEPHANT FIGHT*
Leaf from Padshah–nameh, Indian (Mughal period), c. 1639
Metropolitan Museum of Art, New York 1989.135.

10 *PULCINELLA*
Giovanni Domenico Tiepolo, Italian 1726?–1804
Pen and brown ink, brown wash over black chalk

11 *PIERROT, CALLED GILLES*
Jean-Antoine Watteau, French
Musée du Louvre, Paris. Bequest of Dr. Louis La Caze

13 *THE STROLLING PLAYERS*
Francisco de Goya, Spanish
© Museo del Prado, Madrid

14 *THE LADIES OF THE CARS,* 1885
James Tissot, American
Minneapolis Institute of Art, Minnesota

15 *MISS LA LA AT THE CIRQUE FERNANDO,* 1879
Edgar Degas, French
Reproduced by courtesy of the Trustees, The National Gallery, London

16 *THE STRONG MAN,* 1905
Pablo Picasso, Spanish
Pen and ink over pastel, 12½" x 9½"
The Baltimore Museum of Art: The Cone Collection, formed by Dr. Claribel Cone and Miss Etta Cone of Baltimore, Maryland BMA 1950.12.491

17 *JUGGLERS AT THE CIRQUE FERNANDO,* 1879
Pierre-Auguste Renoir, French
© 1991 The Art Institute of Chicago, Mr. and Mrs. Potter Palmer Collection, 1922. 440

19 *CARNIVAL EVENING,*
Henri Rousseau, French
Philadelphia Museum of Art. The Louis E. Stern Collection

21 *BAREBACK RIDERS,* 1886
W. H. Brown, American
National Gallery of Art, Washington D.C.

22 *THE JUGGLER*
Georges Rouault, French
Color sugarlift aquatint, printed on BFK Rives. Published by Ambrose Vollard in *Cirque*, text by André Suarez.

23 *IN THE CIRQUE FERNANDO: THE RINGMASTER*
Henri de Toulouse-Lautrec, French
© 1992 The Art Institute of Chicago. Joseph Winterbotham Collection 1925.523.

25 *THE CIRCUS,* 1891
Georges Seurat, French
Musée D'Orsay © Photo RMN, Paris. Bequest of John Quinn

27 *SOIR BLEU,* 1914
Edward Hopper, American
Collection of Whitney Museum of American Art, New York. Josephine N. Hopper Bequest 70.1208. Photography Robert E. Mates, New Jersey

28 *LINA PANTZER,* 1915
George Grosz, German
Pencil, 11¹⁰⁄₁₆" x 9". Reproduced in *Der Querschnitt*, March 1925

29 *MASQUERADE,* 1922
Karl Hofer, German
Museum Ludwig, Cologne © Rheinisches Bildarchiv

31 *CLOWN ON A HORSE,* 1927
Marc Chagall, Russian
Courtesy Herbert Black, Montreal

32 *THE WHITE CLOWN,* 1929
Walt Kuhn, American
Oil on canvas, 40¼" x 30¼"
© 1993 National Gallery of Art, Washington D.C.
Gift of the W. Averall Harriman Foundation in memory of Marie N. Harriman

33 *PIP AND FLIP,* 1932
Reginald Marsh, American
Courtesy Terra Museum of American Art, Chicago, Daniel J. Terra Collection.

34 *PERFORMING TIGER,* 1934
John Steuart Curry, American
10½" x 14"
Courtesy ACA Galleries, New York

35 *THE FLYING CODONAS,* 1932
John Steuart Curry, American
Collection of the Whitney Museum of American Art, New York, Purchase 33.10
Photography by Geoffrey Clements, New York

37 *THE CHARIOT RACE,* 1933
Milton Avery, American
Courtesy Grace Borgenicht Gallery, New York

38 *CIRCUS TUMBLERS*
Ben Shahn, American
© 1993 VAGA, New York

39 *ACROBAT ON TRAPEZE,* 1940
Max Beckmann, German
The Saint Louis Art Museum, Bequest of Morton D. May

40 *ELEPHANT ACT,* 1937
Robert Riggs, American
Lithograph, 14¼" x 19½"

41 *CIRCUS ELEPHANTS,* 1941
John Marin, American
© 1991 The Art Institute of Chicago, Alfred Stieglitz Collection, 1949.609

42 *THE CONCERT*
Jean Dufy, French
Oil on canvas, 15" x 18"
Courtesy ACA Galleries, New York

43 *THREE CLOWNS IN A RING,* 1944
George Schreiber, American
The Metropolitan Museum of Art, New York
George A. Hearn Fund, 1945

44 *CIRCUS PERFORMER ON A BALANCED BALL,* 1930
Yasuo Kuniyoshi, American
Lithograph, 14⅛" x 10¼"
Archives of American Art 1949

45 *CLOWN WITH A PIGEON,* 1989
Krishna Reddy, Indian
Courtesy of the artist